For my grandmother, Bea, with love —BB

To my hubby, Steve
Excited to share a lifetime of firsts with you —HH

ABOUT THIS BOOK

The illustrations for this book were done digitally. This book was edited by Deirdre Jones and designed by Véronique Lefèvre Sweet. The production was supervised by Patricia Alvarado, and the production editor was Lindsay Walter-Greaney. The text was set in ShagExpert Lounge, and the display type is Chauncy DeCafMedium.

• Little, Brown and Company • Hachette Book Group • 1290 Avenue of the Americas, New York, NY 10104 • Visit us at LBYR.com • First Edition: February 2021 • Little, Brown and Company is a division of Hachette Book Group, Inc. • The Little, Brown name and logo are trademarks of Hachette Book Group, Inc. • The publisher is not responsible for websites (or their content) that are not owned by the publisher. • Library of Congress Cataloging-in-Publication Data • Names: Birdsong, Bea, author. | Hatam, Holly, illustrator. • Title: Sam's first word / by Bea Birdsong ; illustrated by Holly Hatam. • Description: First edition. | New York : Little, Brown and Company, 2021. | Audience: Ages 4-8 | Summary: Baby Sam is ready to say her first word, but the adults in her life keep missing her pronouncement. • Identifiers: LCCN 2019031256 | ISBN 9780316452441 (hardcover) | ISBN 9780316452434 (ebook) | ISBN 9780316452410 • Subjects: CYAC: Babies—Fiction. | Speech—Fiction. • Classification: LCC PZ7.1.B5427 Sam 2021 | DDC [E]—dc23 • LC record available at https://lccn.loc.gov/2019031256 • ISBNs: 978-0-316-45244-1 (hardcover), 978-0-316-45243-4 (ebook), 978-0-316-45242-7 (ebook), 978-0-316-45245-8 (ebook) • PRINTED IN CHINA • APS • 10 9 8 7 6 5 4 3 2 1

Sam's First Word

By **Bea Birdsong**

Illustrated by
Holly Hatam

L **B**
Little, Brown and Company
New York Boston

There once was a newish baby. Her name was Sam.

Sam could do many things.

She could wave her arms . . .

. . . and clap her hands . . .

. . . and take off her diaper.

The big people in Sam's family were always excited when she did something new.

They smiled.

They laughed.

They cheered.

And they wondered what she'd do next.

"Perhaps she will say her first word," they said.

I hope it will be Mr. Theotopolous!

said Mr. Theotopolous.

He was their next-door neighbor.

"POOP," said Sam.

But no one paid any attention. They were busy thinking about how to get what they wanted.

"I will sing a song for Sam," said Mama.

Mama's song had sixty-three words.
All of them were *Mama*.

"POOP," said Sam.

She waved her arms to get Mama's attention.
But Mama was too busy singing.

"I will tell Sam a story," said Papa.

Papa's story had 203 words.
All of them were *Papa*.

"POOP," said Sam.

She clapped her hands to get Papa's attention.
But Papa was too busy telling his story.

"I will paint a picture for Sam," said Nana.

She painted *Nana* eighty-six times on the living room wall.

"POOP," said Sam. She pointed to her diaper.

Nana didn't pay any attention because she had just remembered that Sam couldn't read.

"I will recite a poem for Sam," said Mr. Theotopolous.

His poem had forty-four words.
Twenty-two of them were *Mister*.
The other twenty-two were
Theotopolous.

But Sam didn't pay any attention. She was busy
thinking about how to get what *she* wanted.

She had tried waving
her arms.

She had tried clapping
her hands.

There was only one
thing left to do.

Sam announced.

Mama stopped singing.
Papa stopped talking.
Nana stopped painting.

Mr. Theotopolous kept reciting his poem, but he lowered his voice.

She laughed.

She cheered.

And she wondered what she'd say next....